·THE NOSEY PARKERS CLUB·

HAPPY GO LUCKY

Written by
Judy Folk

Illustrations by
Bryan Ballinger

1st

Permissions Department
NP Publishing
3311 W. Clearwater Avenue, Suite B130
Kennewick, WA 99336

Text copyright © 2006 by J.A. Folk
Illustrations copyright © 2008 Bryan Ballinger
All rights reserved.
Published in the United States 2008 by NP Publishing.

www.noseyparkers.com

First Edition
Printed in Korea

ISBN: 978-0-9820526-0-0

Get ready to fall in love with The Nosey Parkers! Join them as they solve problems, help others, and learn the true meaning of friendship and acceptance. Each member of the Nosey Parker Club has a unique and heartwarming story to share with you.

Read about the Nosey Parkers at www.noseyparkers.com.

Happy Go Lucky

Halley's Halo

Nobody's Perfect

Sarge and the Silver Whistle

Winston Finds His Way

Lucky the dachshund lived in Sunnyside. He had shiny, reddish brown hair, a long straight nose, a long body and very short legs. Lucky and his friends, the Nosey Parkers, met at the dog park every Saturday morning. They played on the K-9 agility course; it had jumps to jump over, poles to weave in and out of, and bright colored plastic tubes to crawl through.

Lucky's favorite part of the park was the oval race track. He spent hours and hours racing around the track. The Nosey Parkers called him the lean, mean, running machine.

He could run like the wind!

Lucky loved competing in dog races and the Nosey Parkers loved watching him run. They would cheer and wave shiny red and gold flags that said Lucky Dog Pit Crew.

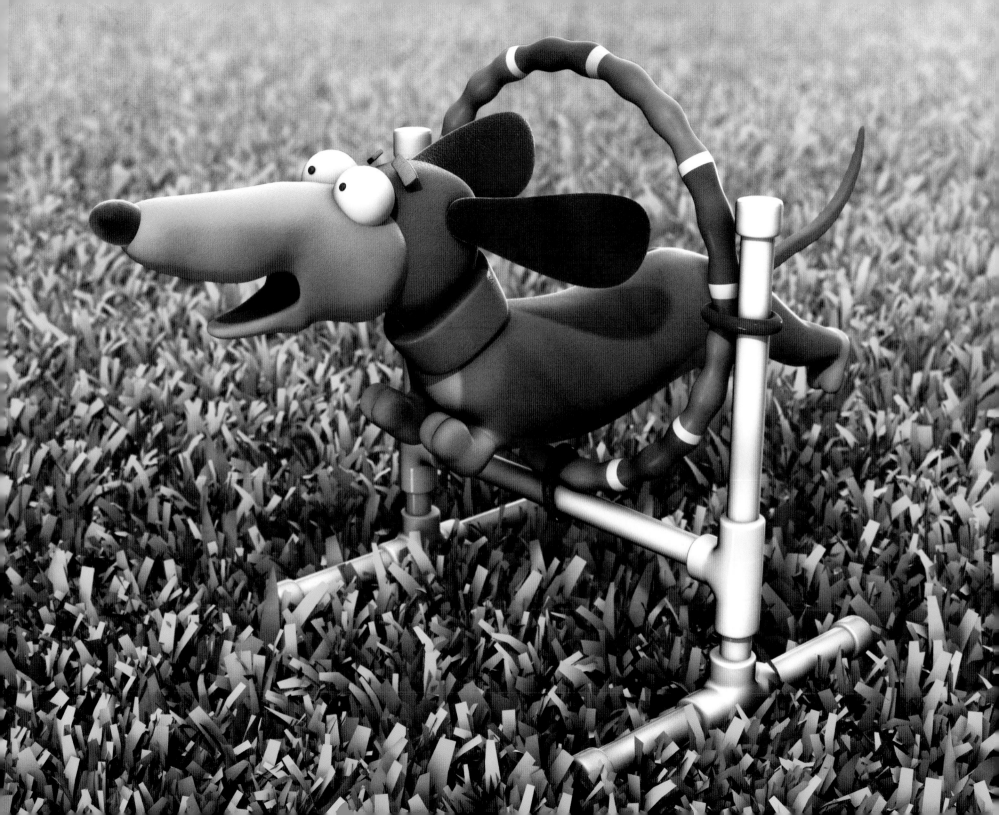

One fateful afternoon, the Nosey Parkers were at the park waiting for the races. Lucky finished stretching, bending, and warming up for his first race.

He trotted over to the Pit Crew. They gave him "high fours" with their paws and wished him good luck. The race was about to start. Lucky lined up with the other dachshunds at the starting gate.

On your mark, get set, go!

The dachshunds were off and running around the track. They ran faster and faster and faster. The finish line was just ahead. *Lucky was in the lead!*

The Nosey Parkers cheered wildly as Lucky crossed the finish line.

He won, he won!
Way to go, Lucky!

"Boy, you really smoked those other wieners! You ran so fast, those other dogs looked like they were standing still," barked Paco, the Mexican hairless dog. "You're the big dog now!" woofed Winston, the English bulldog.

Lucky walked around panting and catching his breath. He felt like he was on top of the world!

The next race was about to start. The dogs lined up at the gate.

On your mark, get set, go!

The dogs raced around the track in a whirl of dust. Lucky was running as fast as he could. He felt like he was flying, his ears back, cheeks flapping in the wind. Just as he rounded the last corner, Lucky's feet got tangled up with the dog running just behind him. Both dogs tumbled onto the track.

! ! ! ! ! Oh no! ! ! ! !

Everyone waited to see if the two dogs were okay. The second dog got up slowly. He was shaken up, but appeared to be all right.

Lucky was still lying on the track. He hadn't moved at all. The veterinarian, Dr. Ginger Snap, ran onto the track. She knelt down beside Lucky—he was breathing—but he was not awake. Lucky was unconscious.

Dr. Ginger Snap carefully put Lucky onto the stretcher and took him to her animal hospital. The Nosey Parkers gasped!

Will Lucky be alright??

The Nosey Parkers went home and waited for news about Lucky.

While they waited, they made get well cards with pictures of dog bones, fetching sticks, Frisbees, and colorful bouncing balls. In the morning they took the cards to the animal hospital for Lucky.

The next Saturday, the Nosey Parkers met again in the park. They were hoping Lucky would be there, but no Lucky. Instead, Dr. Ginger Snap was there. "Hello everyone," she said in her warm, but serious voice. "I know you are very worried about your friend Lucky.

"I wanted to come and tell you that Lucky loves the cards you made for him. I also wanted to tell you how he is doing.

"Lucky is awake now and feeling much better, but he was badly injured in that accident. When he fell, he broke his back and hurt his spinal cord. Lucky can't move his back legs."

When will Lucky be able to move his back legs?

"Well, Winston, it's very sad." Dr. Ginger Snap continued, "Lucky will not be able to move his back legs ever again. But he'll be going home soon and he would love to see all of you."

The Nosey Parkers felt very sad. They lay down in the grass and thought about Lucky. Paco let out a long sigh and said, "Poor Lucky! He loves to run more than any dog in the whole world."

Now what will he do?!?

Winston's ears perked up when he heard children playing on top of the hill. He watched as one girl walked on her hands while the other girl held her feet up. Winston thought the girls looked just like a wheelbarrow being pushed down a hill. "That looks fun," thought Winston.

Then he spotted a horse trotting up the park lane. The horse was pulling a two-wheeled cart. Clip-clop, clip-clop, clip-clop went the horse's hooves. Winston stared at the horse-drawn cart as it passed by the Nosey Parkers.

Hey, I have an idea!

Winston barked excitedly, "Wheels! What if Lucky had wheels? He could use his front legs like those children playing on the hill, and his back legs can rest on a cart with wheels."

Paco yapped excitedly, "My uncle Hector could help us! He can build anything!"

Paco took the Nosey Parkers to meet Uncle Hector. "This is my Uncle Hector! He fixes cars, revs up motorcycles and does totally sweet paint jobs on hot rods." The Nosey Parkers described the cart they wanted for Lucky. "Can you make the cart, Uncle Hector?" asked Paco.

"Of course I can," he said. "When the cart is finished, you and your friends can paint it." Everyone wagged their tails.

"What color are you going to paint the cart?" asked Uncle Hector. "Red and gold, because those are our club colors!" woofed Winston. "We'll paint lightning bolts and put Lucky's name on it."

That sounds great! Let's get to work!

Uncle Hector was a fast builder. In no time at all, the cart was done.

Now it was time for the Nosey Parkers to paint Lucky's new cart. They worked fast and furious … late into the night.

The next morning Uncle Hector opened the door to his shop and heard loud snoring. Winston and the other Nosey Parkers lay sound asleep on the floor. Uncle Hector turned on the lights.

Rise and shine, sleepyheads!

There in front of him was a beautiful sight! The Nosey Parkers were covered from the tip of their noses to the tip of their tails with red and gold paint. Right beside them stood the cart, all painted and ready to go.

"Wow! You did a great job. Lucky's ride looks really cool!" said Uncle Hector. The Nosey Parkers grinned.

Two weeks later, Lucky was well enough to go home. He was excited to see his friends again. Lucky spotted the Nosey Parkers heading up the street toward his house.

Here they come!

"We sure missed you," yapped Paco. Everyone was thrilled to see Lucky again. Lucky thanked his friends for the beautiful cards.

He felt happy and sad at the same time. Lucky was happy to see his friends but sad that he couldn't run and jump with them anymore.

"Umf, umf," Winston cleared his throat and said, "Lucky, we have a welcome home surprise for you…" Uncle Hector walked up pulling the cart.

"What's this?" Lucky asked. Uncle Hector explained, "Winston had this wonderful idea that a pull-cart like this might help you walk using just your front legs. Your friends asked me to build it for you and here it is." Lucky was overwhelmed.

My goodness, my goodness!

"Come on Lucky, try it out," said Winston, as he lifted Lucky up.

Wait, wait! Please stop!

"Lucky, what's wrong?" Winston asked.

Lucky held on tight to Winston's neck and whispered into his ear, "I don't want to try it. I'm scared."

Winston rubbed his nose against Lucky's nose. "I know you're scared, but we can do this together," said Winston.

Lucky stared into Winston's gentle brown eyes for a long time. Then he took a deep breath and said, "Okay… I'll try."

Winston carefully set Lucky in the cart then he snuggled beside him while Uncle Hector adjusted the harness.

Uncle Hector tinkered and tweaked the cart and harness until everything fit perfectly. "There, you're all set to go," said Uncle Hector. "Give it a try, just take a step."

Lucky looked over at Winston. Winston smiled and gave the paws up sign. Lucky took one step… then another… and then another.

The cart rolled smoothly beneath his back legs. The Nosey Parkers barked and jumped up and down with excitement.

He's walking! He's walking! ! !

The Nosey Parkers walked beside Lucky as he went around the track. He walked very slowly at first, then a little faster until he was actually trotting. Lucky could hardly believe it! He could walk and move again. Maybe he could even race again. He felt like himself again, happy-go-Lucky.

The accident changed his life in a way he could never have imagined—now, because of his friends, his life had changed again!

A few weeks later, Lucky stood at the starting line in his bright red and gold cart. Lucky and the other dogs with carts were ready to race.

"On your mark, get set, go!" shouted the announcer. The dogs were off and running fast around the track.

Lucky ran faster and faster as the Lucky Dog pit crew cheered.

! ! ! Go, Lucky, go! ! !

The Nosey Parkers howled and jumped for joy as Lucky crossed the finish line. He had won the race!

Lucky proudly wheeled himself into the winner's circle. The judge pinned a big blue ribbon on his collar as the crowd roared! Then Lucky trotted over to the sidelines where all of his friends were cheering for him. His eyes glistened with happy tears. "You did something wonderful, thank you!" said Lucky, licking their faces. Now everyone had happy tears!

Lucky took his big blue ribbon off and put it on Winston's collar. "This ribbon belongs to you, Winston," Lucky said. "With you and the other Nosey Parkers as my friends, I really am a lucky dog … the luckiest dog in the world!"

From that day on, Uncle Hector made carts for paralyzed animals and Lucky taught them how to use their new wheels.

Lucky even started a racing club for paralyzed pets. And what did he call it?

Freewheeling Friends!

Happy Go Lucky is the story of a wiener dog who was born to run.

ISBN: 978-0-9820526-0-0